To Mrs. Van Vleck. Thanks for pushing me into the spotlight and helping me to see how big my dreams could be once I started believing in myself.

-Ian

To all the friends who encouraged me, and believed in me when I didn't believe in myself. Special thanks to my husband and my mother. Without your support, these illustrations would never have been finished. Finally, Ian: thank you so much for giving me the opportunity to realize a dream! We did it!

-Teshura

Special Thanks:

Michael McKinney, Melissa Cypress Pagonis, Ann and Bob Holmquist, Matthew Bigelow, Heath Farrell, Cindy Sperry, Aaron Lewis, Justin Noormand, Douglas Thrift, Paige Farrell, Steve and Marni Engh, Don Fitz-Roy, Jax Strobel, Stephanie Wilton, Jaysree Joseph-Cabral, Steven Shulem, Timothy Foutz, and Brian Pressler.

King For A Night

Requests for permission to make copies of any part of the work should be submitted online at info@mascotbooks.com or mailed to Mascot Books, 560 Herndon Parkway #120, Herndon, VA 20170.

PRT0615A

Printed in the United States

ISBN-13: 978-1-63177-000-5
Library of Congress Control Number: 2015902740

www.mascotbooks.com

King for a Night

FOR A Night

Ian Foutz

Illustrations by Ipo Teshura Casil-Goodman

Elliot was happiest when he was reading books about dinosaurs, eating cake, or hanging out with his best friend Jackie.

His classmates Miguel and Shawn, though, were happiest when Elliot's glasses were broken, his books were torn, or his eyes were red.

It had been that way since first grade. But one day, all of that changed.

"It's time for our class play," Mrs. Taylor said. "This year, we will perform *The Emperor's New Clothes*."

Miguel would be the Emperor, of course. As for Elliot, he would be a tree, a rock, or a horse. Everyone knew that.

Everyone but Mrs. Taylor, who picked Elliot to be the Emperor.
Jackie squealed, Elliot groaned, and Miguel, for once, didn't say
anything at all.

Elliot was quiet the entire bus ride home. How could he be Emperor? He'd never even led the lunch line before!

His parents cheered when he told them the news. His sister Sonia had a different reaction, and a question. "Doesn't the Emperor have to walk around in his *underwear*?"

Underwear?!? He couldn't even take his shirt off at the beach!

Elliot thought of Miguel and Shawn and hung his head. Not even a T-Rex would be able to save him when this was over.

He tried to think of a way out of his mess, but a certain first grader kept distracting him.

Elliot worked hard to convince Mrs. Taylor that someone, *anyone* would be a better Emperor. He even pretended to lose his voice, but nothing worked. Every time he asked, she just smiled and said, "Don't worry, Elliot. I have faith in you."

If she did, then she was the only one.

Miguel tried to mess Elliot up during every rehearsal. Jackie, his Empress, cheered him on. Even when he sang like a stuffed-up hippo.

Elliot laughed when he saw Miguel's jester costume for the first time.

Then he saw his own, and his face turned almost as red as his hair.

But when Jackie draped the royal coat over his shoulders, boxers and bunny slippers didn't seem so scary anymore.

Acting was hard.

Elliot kept tripping, walking into doors, and forgetting his lines. Miguel and Shawn told him to just give up.

He almost did, but in the end he decided that he couldn't let Jackie or Mrs. Taylor down.

Even though he knew that, no matter how hard he tried, he would never be good enough.

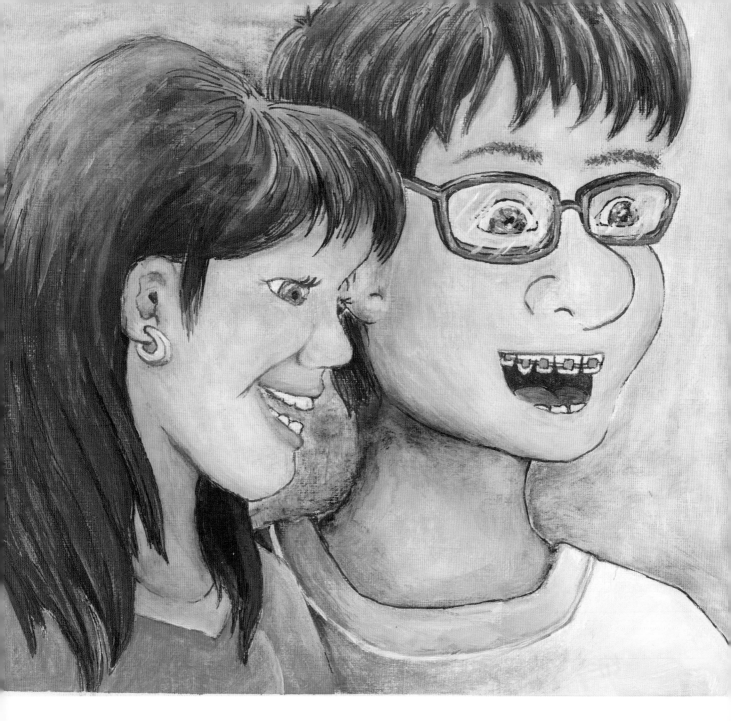

One day, while studying for a history test, Elliot realized something. Memorizing lines was really no different than remembering all those names and dates.

Maybe he could do this after all.

Elliot went to go tell his mom, but got distracted when he saw his dad stomping around like a royal triceratops. When Dad tripped over the cape, Elliot smiled.

If a royal triceratops could make mistakes, then so could he.

Elliot began wearing his cape to school. It was a hit with everyone. Well, *almost* everyone.

One day, Shawn stole the cape and threw it in the mud. Elliot smelled like sweaty socks for the rest of the week.

He didn't care. Emperors fought wars all the time. It was part of their job.

"The show must go on," he told Jackie. "Even if this thing does need a wash. Or twenty."

Besides, there was no time for laundry. All of Elliot's free time was spent with Jackie, singing and rehearsing his lines until his tongue needed a two-week vacation.

Sonia kept saying he looked like a moldy piece of bread, but something told Elliot she was just jealous.

He could feel a difference. The cape had transformed him, and now there was no going back.

At last, the final rehearsal came. They would perform the play twice, and Elliot was still nervous. Miguel's dangerous smiles didn't help, either.

Practice ended, and Elliot put his cape away with a gulp. Tomorrow would come whether he wanted it to or not. All he could do was cross his fingers and hope for a miracle. Or a meteor.

The first performance started off great. Elliot remembered all of his lines, and Miguel forgot most of his. But disaster struck in the final scene, and Miguel was quick to make use of his props.

Elliot closed his eyes to shut out the crowd's laughter. His crown rolled offstage, and he wished he could do the same. Run right off the stage, and never come back.

Elliot couldn't sleep. When his door squeaked open, he dried his eyes and pretended to snore.

"I know you can't hear me," Sonia said. "But you're not bread. Or moldy. You're stinky and you trip a lot, but you're the Emperor. And you're better than Miguel any day."

The door closed, and Elliot felt his heart swell.

Emperors fought wars all the time. This time, he was going to win.

Heart-covered boxers and all.

Elliot kept bowing even after the curtain closed. When Shawn grinned and Miguel gave him a high-five, Elliot's smile grew three sizes larger.

He felt like he was dreaming. When Mrs. Taylor called his name, he blinked twice, turned around, and got pulled into a hug.

"I knew you could do it," she said.

"Me too," Elliot said, squeezing her just a little too tight. "Me too."

(photo by Spencer Shulem, 2012)

About the Author

Ian Foutz is a 5th Grade teacher in Oxnard, California. He loves putting on class plays, not getting hit in the face with pies, and imagining what it would be like to ride a T-Rex to school one day.

This is his second book after *Year of the Dragon*.